TITLE

THE SANTA'S MAGIC

Chapter 1

Out of the relative multitude of young ladies that Nick Christmas might have picked, he picked me, the bashful no one who minded my own business. Nothing phenomenal at any point occurred at Port Sunshine High. Not until Nick showed up. I was astonished he even seen me. No other person at any point had. We'd been dating for a very long time, and I felt lighter than air at whatever point we kissed. He and I had discussed making the following stride, yet we chose to delay until Prom. We needed it to be awesome, booking a lodging where we could go through the night together. My mother and his uncle would throw a tantrum in the event that they knew what we were arranging, however we stayed quiet about it, and presently the night had come.

Here we are, together at Prom. The council had attacked the craftsmanship office, utilizing a revolting measure of hued paper. It took them weeks to make sufficient paper blossoms to cover the exercise center corridor. Glade backgrounds lined the dividers, and they dressed the tables with white material fabrics, and dressed the seats in shaded organza bows, befitting of a warm summer's day. I adored it. Or then again perhaps the reality I was infatuated had elevated my state of mind. Scratch looks crazy in his dark tux and dress shoes, his brownish hair slicked back in a refined style. I continue to squeeze myself on the off chance that this is a fantasy. I'm dressed like the fantasy princesses I used to find out about, the precious stones on my light blue outfit sparkles underneath the lights. Scratch . . . the kid with ethereal blue eyes, with a grin as brilliant as a fresh winter's day, whirls me around in his arms as we dance to our melody. My heart is pulsating almost too fast to measure. I can't really accept that how awesome this feels at the present time.

Scratch appeared suddenly, enlisting at Port Sunshine High during our senior year. Young ladies attempted to stand out enough to be noticed, yet he didn't show any interest in them—with the exception of me. I felt it from the absolute first day as he strolled to the vacant work area adjacent to mine, that there was a sparkle between us. It was practically otherworldly like Cupid struck a bolt through my heart and presently Nick was everything I could ponder. He has the lightest blue eyes, practically polar white. I knew right then that I needed to know this person. I needed to discover where he came from and why. There's a traditional thing about the manner in which Nick seems as though he has been moved from somewhere else, from some other time, straight out of a Dickens novel and into the cutting edge world.

He doesn't act like every other person. For an attractive person, he isn't presumptuous like the athletes, yet he's not actually a geek all things considered. He knows things. Things normal folks neglect. He's enchanting, kind, and appears to be somewhat credulous at times. Particularly with regards to confiding in others. Not every person means well. They like to ridicule Nick, and that infuriates me. He's a sweet person who sees the best in everybody. Before he came here, Nick was self-taught. I thought perhaps his folks were teachers since he talks like a researcher. He cherishes pretty much everything. At whatever point I watch him, it resembles he's encountering things for the absolute first time.

The music stops, and Nick grins at me. He holds me as though I'm delicate like he's apprehensive I may break. "Much thanks to you for going with me to Prom," Nick says, and I can feel the delight exuding from him. It basically illuminates the room.

I laugh. "Scratch, you're my beau. Who else could I go with?"

Scratch shakes his head, grinning. "At the point when I came here, I didn't have the foggiest idea what's in store. I didn't anticipate viewing as this

My heart vacillates, trusting he feels the same way as I do. We haven't said the "L" word yet. We need to mean it when we say it. "What did you find?" I ask, provoking him to let me know what he implies by that.

Scratch cocks his head aside and his lips idiosyncrasy as he might suspect. "You," he says, and I nearly fail to remember where I am briefly. He holds me around my midsection and pulls me closer. We're both radiating as he leans his brow against mine.

"I preferred you as soon as I looked at you," he admits. "I realized you were the best one for me."

The one for him.

"Scratch—" I stammer, frantic to exclaim everything and let him know how I feel.

He kisses me and the world melts away around us. He lifts me and spins us around on schedule for the melody to change. This one has a quicker beat, and my feet are beginning to hurt in my gem encrusted siphons. They're not much, simply something I got in the deals around Christmas time.

"Would you like to leave and registration at the inn?" Nick asks, seeing me jump as he puts me down on my feet.

I gesture, then, at that point, remove my shoes and walk shoeless to Nick's vehicle. He drives an unobtrusive Volvo that she imparts to his uncle. His folks live and work abroad, yet he doesn't delve into insights concerning what it is that they do. All I know is that they run a toy processing plant some place. He came here to acquire some valuable experience as opposed to being cooped up miles from progress—or whatever that implied.

Scratch drives us to the inn, and I'm happy when he actually looks at us in, so I can drop down on the enormous four-banner bed like a starfish. My head is turning and my stomach shudders with anxiety. Scratch's anxious as well. His hands are shaking as he drinks water from a container. I get up to look at how crazy this room is. I'm not even certain how Nick could bear the cost of this. I came here with zero assumptions, however presently I'm so overpowered. The indented hot tub on the overhang is foaming endlessly, and I strip down to my clothing, having not carried a two-piece to change into. Nobody can see us from far up here, so I don't mind as I shout to Nick, advising him to move past here and go along with me.

Scratch makes off his garments and strides out through the sliding entryways. The sun is setting not too far off in a combination of blues, cloudy orange, and red with cushioned white fly streams where planes have run into each other. I'm feeling so hummed at the present time. My man sinks down next to me wearing only his clothing with a wolfish grin, and the sight alone is sufficient to drive a holy person to sin. I need him, and I'm finished pausing. Scratch inclines in to kiss me and I ride his hips, warming things up an indent since we haven't seen underneath our garments up to this point. His slender body has the smallest muscle definition from playing physical games. I like what I see, and I show him however much I kiss him back. Scratch mishandles at my bra catch, however at that point it unfastens as I go to help. He throws the bra onto the floor alongside the tub, and we wriggle out of our briefs, feeling only warm skin as our stripped bodies slide together, his erection sandwiched between us, crushed against my stomach.

"Will I proceed to get a condom?" Nick asks, his eyes flicking to and fro between mine, looking for explanation.

I shake my head, expecting to feel him inside me, exposed and crude, similar to the manner in which God planned. "No, it'll be fine. I'll take off assuming you let me know when," I say, and he gestures in understanding.

We have most of the night to investigate what makes us quiver and wriggle. It's still very early, and we don't anticipate dozing a lot. I read some place that doing it in the water makes things more straightforward the initial time. Scratch stresses over harming me, and mumbles that I ought to go gradually. I lift a bit and incline in, situating his rooster where I really want it, feeling the sharp sting as the engorged head blasts through my virgin opening. My pussy ignites with fight, extending wide to oblige him. Scratch's pretty much as hard as a stone, and we shout out as I sink downward on him. My midsections consume where our hips meet. I'm full so loaded with Nick; it damages to move. My body shakes as I trust that the fire will calm down.

"I love you," he tells me, and reality inside those cold eyes adds substance to his words. He would not joke about this. He truly would not joke about this. Scratch Christmas loves me. A cry gets in my throat as I let that get comfortable.

"I love you, as well," I answer, tracking down the solidarity to move finally.

I grind my hips and he skips his, finding a musicality we both appreciate. It feels excessively great, and we're overwhelmed by a frisson of fervor, allowing energy to muffle all presence of mind. Everything I can feel is Nick, and I'm suffocating in happiness. I shiver and shake as I cum, and he barks out a cruel cry, snapping his hips in vertical pushes. I feel him beating inside me, his face reshaping with happiness.

"Goodness, Holly," Nick moans my name in the phosphorescence of our lovemaking. "That was stunning."

It doesn't happen to us how foolish we're being. We're excessively youthful and stupid to understand the outcomes of our activities, accepting the juvenile hypothesis that the initial time doesn't count. I'm excessively head over heels and desire to pause and figure what could occur.

Chapter 2

Holly and I have intercourse long into the early hours, and it's the greatest evening of my life. To think, I was hesitant to leave the North Pole and enlist at a customary secondary school. My folks demanded I experience an ordinary life in light of the fact that soon the decision would be taken from me. I needed to satisfy my family heritage, and as Santa's grandson, there was no getting away from it. The sorcery had outperformed my dad and showed inside me. I was the successor to the studio, the elven realm, the flying sled, the enchanted reindeer, and the feared list. Those were a few shoes to fill, just like the red suit, which would need to be changed to fit me. Grandpa had a soft spot for eating an excessive number of treats while doing his rounds. He used to joke that I would develop into the suit, however I didn't need an immense gut to cushion it out with.

Since I've invested energy here at Port Sunshine, it moves me to switch things around at home. The old ways have functioned admirably, yet the world is advancing, and individuals are beginning to fail to remember the genuine significance of Christmas. My family attempted to adjust as toymakers, just as running the best circulation administration the world has at any point seen. Not to gloat, but rather my grandpa can zoom all over the planet in one evening, conveying presents to each family. I couldn't imagine anything better than to see Jeff Bezos do that without anyone else.

"Scratch?" Holly murmurs as we cuddle in bed. "Could it be said that you are conscious?"

I mumble and kiss the side of her head. "Is everything alright? Do you really want me to make you something?"

I feel her grin against my chest. "No, I was simply pondering what we'll do later we graduate."

My heart shocks with the real world, realizing I don't have a lot of time left. Holly doesn't be aware of me—regarding who I am. I continue to intend to tell her, yet I'm uncertain how to clarify it. She probably won't really accept that me, then, at that point, I'd be compelled to demonstrate it. Our sorcery isn't something you can neglect. Kids all around the world have professed to hear sleighbells on the rooftop, bizarre sparkling comets in the sky, and frigid impressions on the fire hearth. I can't eradicate her memory however much I can't constrain her not to tell anybody. Assuming she dismisses me, I'll be in a bad way. I made a solemn vow never to uncover my character. Our mystery shields us from the rest of the world. The studio is covered behind a mysterious arch. Nobody from the outside can get in except if we welcome them. My mom was the last untouchable to be welcomed when she got drawn in to my dad. More than anything, I needed to carry Holly to my country. I needed to acquaint her with the family. Another explanation they urged me to come here was to track down a reasonable accomplice and I had seen as one My grandpa guaranteed me I would know when I saw her, and I quickly realized that Holly was an ideal young lady for me.

"Better believe it . . . later we graduate," I answer, wincing underneath the shadow of dusk.

There are barely an adequate number of grains in the mystical hourglass to go on until tomorrow evening. I should get back to illuminate my folks about Holly. Then, at that point, I intend to magically transport back on schedule for the graduation function. I'll need to re-energize the hourglass so I can control a return trip for two. It will require a couple of days to aggregate sufficient sorcery dust. Nowadays, there isn't a plenitude of it to save. Particularly not presently the wizardry is decreasing. Holly adores me. She'll get when I come clean with her with regards to me. It'll be fine.

The Jingle ringers ringtone tolls from my telephone—the particular tone that I use for my grandpa. Holly jolts up in bed to discover where it's coming from, then, at that point, understands it's coming from my telephone by the manner in which it illuminates the room like a Christmas tree.

"Truly?" I hear the entertainment in her voice. "A Christmas ringtone in summer."

I swing my legs up, grabbing my telephone from the end table.

"Hi?" I reply, my voice is croaky with depletion.

My bothered grandpa begins chattering about a family crisis, and I trade the phone to my other ear, not needing Holly to get the discussion. Anything that's off-base, it's terrible enough for him to call me at this profane hour.

"Gramps, dial back and start from the start," I tell him, squeezing the edges of my eyes as I lurch into the restroom.

I flick on the light switch, my garbage swinging uninhibitedly on the grounds that I'm however stripped as the day I seemed to be conceived.

"Scratch, we really want you back here this moment," Grandpa exclaims. "Something is off-base. The snow globe is misfiring. Every one of the names are confusing around on the Christmas list. We're having some significant issues here at HQ. In the event that you don't get back here quickly, you could be stuck there for goodness realizes how long."

"As a matter of fact, I wouldn't fret remaining here a short time longer," I tell him, wanting to purchase additional time with Holly. "I'm certain you and Dad can hold the fortification without me. You have Shinny. I'm certain he can sort out what's happening. You needn't bother with me"Nicolas, presently you pay attention to me," Grandpa snaps, utilizing his Santa voice to admonish some power. "You'll do as I say and return right now, or so help me, Rudolph, I'll magically transport around there and come and get you myself."

13

He would do it as well. It's absolutely impossible that I need him to barge in here and get Holly and me in the buff. It's nearly just about as awful as the time he discovered Buddy pushing a treats stick up his derriere.

"Scratch?!" Holly shouted to me. "Is it true that you are OK in there, child?"

Heavenly trinkets.

I cover the speaker with my thumb, hearing my grandpa interest to realize who I'm with.

"Simply a second!" I answer cautiously. "Try not to come in here, darling."

"Nicolas Christmas, I interest to know who's there with you. It's three AM. You better not be at a party, youngster!" Grandpa thunders, not sounding dazzled by any means.

I hear him down the line, hollering at Shinny to tell Bernard, my phony uncle, to get together and returned home. Then, at that point, he demands that I'm to be shipped home promptly, and in a situation of frenzy, I grab a towel from the warmed rail and use it to cover my humility. My skin shivers like I'm being stimulated done with sparkle, and afterward instantly of splendidly shaded lights, I wind up remaining in my granddad's office at the studio. Mysterious residue particles gleam around me like the brilliant sparkle specks from a hello card. I'm 1,000,000 miles from Holly. My first love who I've left abandoned, alone in a lodging room.

Gah! She's never going to excuse me for this.

Grandpa is wearing his red and green holly print night robe—in light of the fact that my life is unexpected like that. His eyes bug out of their attachments as he takes in my tousled appearance. Bernard jumps in a quiet expression of remorse since he realizes where I've been and can think about the thing we've been doing, and Shinny projects me a critical grimace.

"What in the Northern Lights are you wearing?" Grandpa asks, wrinkling his nose with examination. "Is that a Plaza Hotel Towel?"

As yet fastening my telephone between my fingers, I gesture timidly. "It is." I don't have the foggiest idea what else to say, I'm too humiliated to even consider being gotten short like this.

Grandpa snaps his head back with a dazed scowl. "It's somewhat late to be scrubbing down, right?"

I'm not having this discussion. It's past the point of no return—or early—however you take a gander at it, and I'm extremely tired to heck, and I simply need to return to my sweetheart and crash out for the evening. I don't possess energy for this. Me being here will meddle with my arrangements—and ugh! I nibble my clench hand since I recollect what Grandpa told me before he hauled my butt back here—that I'm stuck here until we can sort out a method for sending me back.

"She will dump me without a doubt," I murmur despairingly.

"Huh?" Grandpa scratches his rugged white facial hair.

I clean my hand over my face, not knowing what the heck I planned to do now. "I said, she will dump me, and I can't say I fault her."

It doesn't make any difference now since it's finished assuming I can't return and clarify things.

"Who?" Grandpa inquires.

"Scratch has a sweetheart called Holly," Bernard illuminates them, adding accentuation to her name. "She's pretty."

"No doubt," I say, hauling my give over my face. "She'll be really annoyed when I don't emerge from the restroom." My voice overflows mockery, and my grandpa's demeanor relax with compassion.

"Gracious, was that who you were with?" he asks, then, at that point, pauses for a minute to draw an obvious conclusion. "You were in a lodging, exposed, alone with a beautiful young lady."

Someone simply kill me, please.

"I trust you were protected." My grandmother, Mary, in a real sense appears unexpectedly and stokes the fire.

She rearranges into the workplace to present to Grandpa some cocoa and a mince pie—at three AM—so you can see the value in why he's evenly tested. Then, at that point, just to re-awaken some old animosity, my folks, Nick and Carol, show up as well. It's a family get-together; they're all here to observe my stroll of disgrace. I check my cell and find that it's totally dead. The charger is in my sack adjacent to the bed where Holly is hanging tight for me to no end. I really want to sort this out and quick. I can't keep her pausing. Time works distinctively inside the vault. A month here resembles a year wherever else, which is the reason our mythical beings are so occupied.

"Grandmother, I love you, yet there is such a mind-bending concept as oversharing, so I'm not going to respond to that." I can't tell her that we had fifty-fifty secured sex. My mom is remaining there, stony-confronted, hanging tight for me to goof. In the event that I lie here in the operational hub, I'll set off the alarms on the underhanded rundown, along these lines, I can neither affirm nor deny it. It's the main proviso that works.

"The error happened a couple of hours prior," Shinny discloses to me. "We don't have the foggiest idea what might have caused it."

"Not accommodating," I protest.

"Until we sort this out, it's undependable for you to stay in the open," Grandpa says. "You're my beneficiary. The world is depending on you to reestablish the enchantment." He signals at the snow globe, and I look into it, needing to see what Holly is doing well at this point.

A whirlwind of snow spins around like a cyclone inside a teacup, then, at that point, the tempest clears, and I see Holly wildly looking around searching for me. She holds the telephone to her ear, leaving me frantic voice messages. My throat consumes without precedent for my life, the vision before me obscures as water spills from my eyes, something I have never experienced.

I know it's futile to attempt to speak with her. She can't hear me. Furthermore except if we can sort out what has happened this evening, I'll be stuck here until the end of time. Just Santa has the ability to leave on Christmas Eve, and until the job passes to me, I can't go anyplace. Chapter 3

Holly

I can't believe he ran out on me. Nick, the sweetest guy in the world, which was now up for debate, has ditched me without saying goodbye. At least if he had broken up with me by text, I would have closure. Instead, he just ghosted me.

I try calling him again, but it goes straight through to his voicemail. Even the texts have a red exclamation mark next to them, proving they didn't send. I'm not sure what happened. One minute, we were fine, and the next, he was gone. Was it something I said? Did I do something wrong? Was the sex not good enough? The first time can be anticlimactic, but it wasn't like that for me. It was perfect. That's why I don't understand.

It gets later, and I replay our conversation in a loop in my head during the cab ride home. There's a gaping hole where my heart used to be, the pain just keeps seeping out and there's nothing I can do to stop it. I'm hoping my mom isn't home when I get there, but as we turn the corner to my street, I see her kneeling at the flower bed, pulling out weeds. She looks up, notices the cab slowing down, then gets up to dust off her gloved hands. Mom greets me with a scowl on her face; the kind of look that tells me she knows I didn't stay at my best friend, Meredith's house last night. As if my day couldn't get much worse. I hand the driver some cash and tell him to keep the change, then brace myself for the lecture of the century.

"You lied to me," Mom chastises me, and I hear the worry in her voice. "You didn't stay at Meredith's house, so where were you? I understand you're eighteen, but if you want to be treated like an adult, you ought to behave like one."

There's no point lying to try and weasel my way out of this. Mom has obviously spoken to Alice, Meredith's mom. That's what happens when my best friend's mom is also best friends with my mom. There can be no secrets. I'm guessing Meredith has been busted too. She also stayed with her boyfriend last night.

"I'm sorry, Mom," I apologize. "It won't happen again."

Mom tosses the weeds that she pulled from the flowerbed onto a pile on the lawn. "You're damn right, it won't happen again," she says firmly. "I can't be worrying that you're not where you say you are. I raised you better than to lie to me. How come Nick didn't bring you home? Where is he, anyway? I want a word with him." The look on my face must say it all because she stops mid-rant and her eyes twitch questioningly. "Did you fight?"

"No, Mom," I say, not knowing what else to say. I'm too upset to tell her the truth. Some truths are better left unspoken. "I'm just going to go upstairs and change," I say, revealing nothing about last night.

That's what I do. I go inside, leaving Mom to finish the weeding.

"I have got a good mind to call at his house," Mom calls after me, "and give him a piece of my mind."

Yeah, me too. That isn't a bad idea.

I swap my Prom gown for a pair of faded jeans and a loose-fitted T-shirt and put on a pair of sneakers. I'm so tender down below, it hurts as I sit down on my ballerina pink comforter and glance around my girly-themed room, realizing my innocence is gone. It disappoints me that I've given it away to someone who doesn't appreciate it, and that makes up my mind. I'm going over to Nick's place and I want to know what his problem is. I'm not letting him take my virginity then dump me like a piece of trash. Hell no!

I brush the snags from my long brown hair and tie it up with a scrunchie. My skin looks blotchy, and my eyes are red from when I cried this morning. I inwardly curse my sorry state, hating how weak and pathetic I look. Okay, so, I'm not the first girl that got duped into bed, and I won't be the last. I had been through a lot in this last year. My dad got sick, then sadly died a month after he was diagnosed with prostate cancer. My life almost fell apart, but then I met Nick, and the world made sense again. This proves that I can bounce back from anything. I'll be fine. I've been through worse. I'm no stranger to heartbreak.

If Nick won't pick up his phone or return my calls, then I'll confront him on his home turf, in front of his uncle if need be. Bernard, Nick's uncle, and guardian had dwarfism. He was the friendliest guy, and he always made me feel welcome whenever I stopped by the house.

I hurry downstairs and glance into the sitting room as I pass the hall. My older sister, Hazel, is sitting on the couch with her earbuds in, listening to music. She doesn't see me because she has her nose buried in a magazine. I dart through the front door, side-stepping around Greg, our miniature Dachshund.

Mom glances up from the shrubs as I storm down the driveway. "Hey, where are you going?" she asks, flinging her hands up exasperatedly.

"Nick's," I tell her the truth this time.

Mom plucks off her gloves, then shoves Greg into the house, and yells through to Hazel, telling her to watch the house while she's gone. I doubt Hazel can hear anything with that new-age rock blasting her eardrums. Mom shuts the door, then she runs to catch up to me.

"Why are you following me?" I yell over my shoulder.

Mom runs to match my strides, then power walks alongside me. "You look mad, so I figured you could use some company."

"I just need to talk to Nick, Mom, I don't need a wing woman," I retort.

Mom huffs, clearly out of breath. "Yeah, you're right. I just need to know what to say to the cops when they start looking for Nick's body."

We clear several blocks before turning onto the street where Nick lives. His house is the middle dwelling— the only one that has a Christmas tree mailbox at the edge of the lawn. At first, I thought it was cute because his last name is Christmas, but now it just seems cheesy. But as I reach his house, I notice the mailbox is gone and the curtains have vanished from the windows. The house appears to be empty, but I know that's impossible because I was just here yesterday, and there was way too much crap to pack up and move in one night.

"Oh?" Mom says, looking as confused as me. "Are you sure this is the right house? It doesn't look like anyone has lived here for years."

I run across the patchy lawn to look through the windows and see nothing but an empty shell of a house. All the furniture is gone. There's nothing left to prove Nick ever existed. Mom catches me in her arms as I stagger back with a sob.

"He's gone," I choke out the words. "He didn't even have the decency to say goodbye to me, he just left."

"There, there, Holly," she says soothingly, rubbing my back. "I'm sure there's a good explanation for this."

I shook my head and the tears rolled down my cheeks. "You don't understand, Mom," I hiccoughed. "I was with him last night."

"I know, sweety," Mom replied, not catching the

meaning behind my words. "They must have hired a removal company. Wow, those guys work fast."

I pulled back and wiped my eyes with the back of my hands, but my nose was like a waterfall of mucus. I turned into a blubbering mess.

"Here, take this," Mom says, pulling a tissue from her pocket.

I dry my tears and use it to blow my nose on. Then I turn away, unable to look my mom in the eyes and face the shame I was feeling. If my father was still alive today, he'd be so disappointed in me.

"You don't get it, Mom." I sigh with defeat. "I was with Nick last night, and now this." I gesture around at the empty house and crumple with emotion.

The realization floods my mom's face and her eyes bulge with surprise.

"Oh, Holly—" Her tone oozes sympathy, and she hugs me.

Four weeks later, I realize that I'm late. Nausea kicks in soon after, and I can't hold anything down. I have everything going for me, having graduated at the top of my class. I get into NYU like I always wanted. My dreams of becoming a journalist are finally happening. But as my chest swells with pride, something else starts to grow in my abdomen. And it keeps getting bigger until my clothes don't fit, and I can't ignore it any longer. I hide behind baggy tops and sweatpants, letting my social life fester in a dark pit of denial. Then it happens. Reality comes back to bite me on the ass as my water breaks during my media class. The cramps are the devil, and I think I'm going to die from the pain. Mom and Hazel get a call from the nurse, and they rush to meet me at the hospital.

After sixteen hours of grueling labor, my son, Nicolas Harper, was born red-faced and screaming as he took his first breath. My little spring lamb. I still, to this day, can't explain why I named him after Nick. From the moment he opened his glacial blue eyes, the same as his father's, it only seemed fitting to honor the man who gave him to me. The nurse wrapped him in a blue bundle, just like a belated Christmas gift, and placed him into my arms. It was love at first sight, just as it was when I first laid eyes on Nick back in high school. As much as I tried to push him to the back of my mind, I knew I'd never be able to. Not now that I had a constant reminder of him.

"He's beautiful," Mom gushes as she snaps pictures of him on her iPhone.

Hazel smiles proudly as she peers down at him in my arms. "I can't believe I'm an aunt. Can I hold him?"

I can't stop smiling as I pass him into her open arms, thrilled that he is repairing the bond between us. Our relationship had strained since our father passed away, but this little guy was bringing us all closer together again.

"I don't know how I'm going to cope," I admit. "I worked so hard to get into NYU, and now I guess I'll have to drop out."

Mom eyes me sharply. "Like hell you'll drop out." She throws my sister a meaningful look, they share a silent exchange, and I'm not sure what to make of it.

Hazel runs our dad's auto shop. Mom was supposed to be starting back at the hair salon full-time instead of cutting our neighbors' hair from home. We ought to be careful with money. Dad's life insurance will run out someday. I feel awful about dropping out and wasting the college fund they set aside for me, but what other choice do I have?

"We're going to juggle the responsibility of taking care of Nicky," Mom tells me.

Nicky. I like it.

"We want to help," Hazel adds, backing up what Mom said. "We're a family. And you're the only one of us who has any brains, so you can't drop out of college. I'm counting on you to pay the bills someday," she jokes.

They smile at me, then Hazel hands Nicky to Mom, and she rocks him in her arms. "You must have been so scared." Mom's eyes shimmer with emotion. "But you're not alone, sweetheart. You've got us to help you."

"Thank you," I tell them, meaning it from the bottom of my heart. "I won't let you down again."

Chapter 4

Nick

For months, I've been trying to pinpoint the cause of the glitch so I can return to Holly. Grandpa refused to let me use the snow globe and lectured me about wasting the magic dust. The diminishing supply was at an all-time low. We barely had enough left to power the sleigh on Christmas Eve.

Thump!

A loud noise scares the bejesus out of me and my eyes snap open, the air stinging them raw. That's when I realize I slept in the mailroom again. My grandpa stands over me with a murderous scowl on his face. It's February. I don't get why he dumped the list in front of me. We just got through our toughest year to date, so I was hoping we could relax until springtime. "Guess what?" Grandpa snaps as if he already knows the answer.

I'm feeling accused of something, but unless he tells me, I'm unsure what I've supposedly done.

I scrub my hand over my face and mash my lips together. "Uh, Christmas has come early?" I answer sarcastically.

Grandpa huffs an annoyed breath and shakes his head. "Honestly, Nick, you should have owned up to it months ago and saved us all the trouble."

"I don't know what you're talking about," I say cluelessly.

Grandpa's face is usually jolly, so I'm shocked to see it twist into an angry snarl as he speaks. "You caused the glitch by making it onto the naughty list," he roars.

My eyes bulge in their sockets. "What?!"

Shinny is here too, and he just stares at me with judgemental eyes. "You had sexual relations outside of wedlock," he says in his squeaky voice, ramming rule number three of the Santa Claus handbook down my throat. "You're supposed to marry her first. Your carelessness could have ruined everything we've built here."

My first reaction was to ask him how he knew about my private life, but I already knew the answer. It was the snow globe. I could tell by the revolted look on their faces, they played back the events of that night.

He sees you when you're sleeping. He knows when you're awake. He knows when you've been bad or good, so be good for goodness' sake.

There was no point in trying to deny it. The snow globe never lies.
"But I didn't ruin things permanently," I reply sheepishly. "Does that mean I can go back to Port Sunshine?"
My grandfather's nostrils flare with outrage. He's dressed in brown britches and a white shirt, but his steel toe-capped boots can still kick my ass all around the North Pole if I'm not careful.
"No, Nicolas Noel Christmas. It does not. Your name is still on the naughty list. It's going to take more than a few good deeds to atone for your behavior. You better start acting like the saint you were born to be, or you'll spend the next four years wrapping presents in the

workshop."

"But what about Holly?" I look at him pleadingly. "Let me go back and propose to her. I'll do anything. I swear, I'll do better. I'll try harder. Just let me go back."

Grandpa's expression softens, but it is soon replaced by sympathy. "I'm sorry, Nick. It's out of my hands. Your travel privileges have been revoked until you're ready to take over from me."

My voice sticks in my throat and all that comes out is a shocked squeak. I could be stuck here for years. My gramps isn't ready to retire yet. The glitch in the list may be fixed, but the huge blip in my life hasn't.

"This is bullshit!" I roar. "You can't keep me here against my will."

Grandpa reaches out to me, but I recoil from his touch as if it burns me. "Nick," he says sorrowfully. "If it was up to me, I would let you go. Your happiness is important to me. You can't leave because the magic is keeping you here. You're my heir. The magic passed to you. It's time to finish your training. Only then will you be free to leave the dome."

"How long will that take?" I ask desperately.

Shinny struggles to meet my gaze, but my grandfather's honest eyes fill with empathy. "It takes as long as it takes," he answers. "You'll know when you're ready."

"Tell him about the other problem," Shinny mentions.

Grandpa shoots Shinny a warning look to silence him and shakes his head. "Let him deal with one thing at a time, for pity's sake."

"Very well," Shinny concedes.

They share a furtive look, then mask their emotions as they turn to me.

"You should eat to keep up your strength," Grandpa suggests. "You've been neglecting yourself lately, and

quite frankly . . . you're looking thin."
I glance down and brush the crinkles from my shirt.
My clothes have been a little loose-fitting lately. It's
been difficult to eat when all I can think about is Holly
– what she's doing – who she's with. The thought of
her being with someone else makes me feel sick to my
stomach.
"Ugh! I hate my life," I groan, driving my fingers
through my hair.
My eyes scrunch so tight, lights flash behind my lids.
This is useless. There's nothing more I can do to speed
things up. Whatever happens, happens. I'm just sorry I
didn't see this coming. My folks never warned me what
could happen, they just told me to go and have fun.
Now I'm hurting, and the one person who can fix it
probably hates my guts. It doesn't get any easier with
each passing month. Time flies when you're having
fun, but it drags its feet when you're miserable.
"You won't always feel this way," Grandpa promises.
"You'll be holding the reins before you know it. Soon,
you'll be so busy with work, you won't have time to
take a shit, never mind anything else. Trust me, your
best days are ahead of you."
We go to breakfast and eat pancakes with the elves.
Grandma gives me double helpings of everything,
which arouses my suspicions because — aren't I
supposed to be on the naughty list? How come I'm
getting preferential treatment? I'm the screw-up
grandson. The guy who almost wrecked things for
everyone. Something is amiss here, but I don't know
what it is. My folks are acting weird.
Grandpa wasn't kidding when he said I would have no
time to think. He worked me like a dog, day and night.
Months turned into years. Four years, to be exact. I had
to shove my feelings aside and work through the ranks

to learn the ropes. First, I helped on the production line next to an honorary elf named Buddy. Then I got promoted to a quality control operative, and from there I progressed to the floor manager of the workshop. Now I've been promoted to the CEO of our retail department.

Grandpa handles the list, and he guards it with his life. Not that I care, because I hate admin work. It means I can turn my attention to growing the company into something great. The world has changed. Parents buy their children specific gifts; they tend to stay clear of the traditional toys we make at the workshop. Kids don't want wooden trikes, spinning tops, and stuffed bears. They want BMXs, PlayStations, and smartphones. We can't produce those here — and if we did, we'd go broke. There's no way we can compete with the retail giants out there in the real world, so my plan is . . . if we can't beat them, we should join them. What better way to disguise ourselves than to hide in plain sight using the Santa brand? Our motto "Sharing is Caring" has captured everyone's attention. As well as ensuring everyone gets something for Christmas, we're donating most of our profits to charity. Not all of it. We still have a business to run, and human staff to pay. I'm excited about this. It feels like I'm doing something good for once.

And it's paying off. According to Gramps, my name is out of the red and into the black, which is excellent news. I've achieved my goal. My grandfather says he's almost ready to retire, but first, he wants to see our new chain of department stores succeed. The good news is, now that my name is off the naughty list, it means I'm free to leave the dome. It's not a coincidence that our flagship store is based in Port Sunshine. It's where I met Holly, so it'll always have a special place in my heart. Bernard is coming with me. He's my assistant, and he's set up a news conference for my return. This is my chance to make my family proud. I'm going to win back my girl, and restore the spirit of Christmas.

Chapter 5

Holly

"Deck the halls! It's Holly Harper," Ray Frost, our Editor-in-Chief, comments as I arrive late to the weekly briefing.

He's the kind of guy who turns your cheeks cherry red with patronizing one-liners, knowing full well that if you retaliate, he'll either fuck you or fire you. I think it's his arrogance that makes him seem hotter than he really is, but that's just primal chemistry. Women often find bastards more appealing because they give off Alpha male vibes. Ray has all that arrogant sexiness going for him. He's naturally blond, with smoldering brown eyes, and I can tell he works out by the way his muscles are gift-wrapped beneath his tight white shirt. His tie is askew as if he's enjoyed an early morning romp in his office. I can see why my female colleagues are so enamored by him, but his bastardry tips the scales to "thanks, but fuck no" for me.

All eyes in the packed-out newsroom land on me, and I stammer a feeble apology, "I'm so sorry. My son's teacher wanted to talk to me about something. It's been a rough start to my morning —"

My four-year-old son is obsessed with Christmas and

32

has disputed the preschool Nativity script. This year, his teacher wants to have Santa visit the baby Jesus. But Nicky pointed out that the birth of Christ predates Santa, and that Miss Littlemore should get her facts straight. I just endured a dressing down in front of all the other preschoolers about teaching my son better manners. Nicky is smart. Much smarter than I give him credit for. He reminds me so much of Nick, it's like he belongs in another place, in a different time, and it scares me.

Ray swishes his hand through the air to silence me. "I'm not interested. Sit down."

I am stunned into silence, and I creep toward the only empty chair around the oval table then drag it out slowly. The irritated frown on my colleagues' faces tells me they don't approve of my tardiness, nor are they interested in my reasons for being late. They don't have kids, so they can't relate to me. I'm the newbie, fresh out of college. I know some people here think I was hired for my looks, and not for my intellect, and that's why I'm finding it hard to make friends.

Ray has fucked his way through the entire female workforce, except for Brenda, the veteran receptionist. She's pushing seventy, and she's been here since Ray's dad was Editor-in-Chief. She won't retire, and Ray treats her like a second grandmother, so she'll leave here in a box. I'm the youngest here, and that makes me fresh meat. Unattainable and not fucking interested, fresh meat. I've worked too damn hard to get here, and I just want to provide for my son. It's just hard being a single mom, juggling a job and a kid, and trying to maintain a household in-between. Mom and Hazel have been great, but I can't rely on them forever. They have their own lives to lead. I moved back home to Port Sunshine to be closer to them, sure, but I signed a five-year lease on an apartment close to the Harbor so that Nicky and I can have our own space. It's not much, but the view isn't bad. I just have to prove my worth to Ray without sleeping my way to the top, and maybe he'll put me in front of the camera. If he doesn't . . . well, I've been fetching coffee long enough to get a job at Starbucks.

Ray puts his hands on the table and leans forward, the action makes his biceps bulge and I'm not the only one who notices. Everyone does. Even the guys have man-crushes on Ray. I avert my eyes and reach for the glass of water in front of me to take a sip. Ray watches me closely through narrow eyes and suddenly I'm paranoid. I worry I have something on my face. So I set down my glass and swipe my hand over my mouth, dusting for crumbs from the croissant I ate on the way over here.

"It's that time of year again," Ray announces, his voice laced with cynicism. "You can't escape it. It's rammed down our throats everywhere we go. *Christmas.*" He makes it sound like a curse word, then adds a shudder to show his distaste. "It's all over the TV, the radio, it's in every fucking store." He gestures at me. "Her name reminds me of it too."
I bristle at that comment.
"And now there's a new chain of toy stores taking the world by force," Ray goes on to say. "They're advertised on every billboard. So, now when I'm stuck in traffic, it's all I can see. Christmas, Christmas, Christmas. Bah fucking humbug."

Jeez, what a Grinch.

I don't realize I'm scowling until Ray throws in, "It seems like you disagree with me, Holly."
All eyes flick my way and put me under the spotlight. "Y-you don't like Christmas?" I state the fucking obvious, and I hear chuckling from around the table. Ray's lips quirk with amusement. "No, Holly. I don't like Christmas. Never have, never will."
I'm not a huge fan because of personal reasons, but Nicky is, and I would never take that away from him. I clear my throat as I prepare to make my statement. "I get that it's stressful, buying gifts while struggling to make ends meet," I say, wanting to put my point across because I feel an urge to defend it from goodness knows where. "But we do it for the kids. Isn't it all about doing something nice for someone else? It should bring out the best in us; we should try to be better people, not just at Christmas, but all year round. I've seen the advertisements, Sharing is Caring, and it's powerful. It hits home. Showing someone that you care is a wonderful thing. Gifts don't have to cost a fortune. It doesn't need to cost anything at all. A good deed can be anything to make someone feel valued. Also, I heard the proceeds from the toy store go to worthy causes. Not all families can afford to buy gifts for Christmas. The Workshop donates most of its proceeds to those families who are struggling. It's a great idea."
Ray's eyebrows disappear beneath his floppy fringe, and I wait for him to yell "get out" or point at me and fire me like he's the boss of The Apprentice, but he doesn't. For some reason, I've piqued his interest. That doesn't sit well with the rest of the crew, and they talk over themselves, picking apart everything I just said to suck up to Ray.
"Okay, everyone out," Ray announces, and I feel my

stomach churn with dread. "All except for you." He points at me, and my worst fears are confirmed. He's going to fire me. I'll never work in this industry again. The crew throws smug smirks at each other, then Ray's top news reporter, Sasha Stone, turns to me with a spiteful cackle. She flicks her red hair over her shoulder and grins. "You're so out of here, new girl." She sounds so sure about that as she flounces out of the room, and winks at Ray.

He looks back at her impassively and doesn't react, reciprocate, or sweet fuck all. This doesn't look good. Ray waits for the last person to leave before closing the door. Then he turns to me and folds his arms in front of his chest. I get up out of my chair because I'm too nervous, I can't stay seated. I drape my purse strap over my shoulder and expect to be told to clear out my desk.

"How old is your kid?" Ray asks, his eyes twitching at his question.

"Four," I reply meekly.

I hate that I sound so weak, but I can't afford to be unemployed this side of Christmas. Oh my God. My rent is due next week, and I still have Nicky's presents to get.

Ray nods as he thinks to himself. "All kids love Santa," he says as if he's just had an epiphany.

"That's right, they do," I agree, and I wonder where he's going with this.

Ray sucks in a breath through his nostrils then shocks me as he smiles. "Then you're the right girl for the job." His tone is a little patronizing, but I'm relieved to hear him say it. "The Workshop is opening their Christmas grotto tomorrow night." Ray's eyes glimmer with the thrill of a great scoop.

"Yeah, I know," I tell him. "I bought Nicky's ticket

weeks ago."

Ray blows into his hands excitedly. "Good," he exclaims, his hands coming together in a single clap that makes me jump. "I want you to go there and interview the staff, find out anything you can about the company, and why they insist on secrecy."

"Why are you so interested in The Workshop if you hate Christmas?" I ask him.

Ray rolls his eyes dramatically. "Because I hate Christmas," he reiterates, and I detect the silent "duh" in his tone. "I heard the CEO thinks of himself as the modern-day Santa, and I want to find out everything I can about this guy. Who he is, where did he come from, and why is he so secretive about the business. There must be more to it than just being nice. I smell corruption. They could be hiding dirty money behind his company, and we're going to expose the truth." He catches the doubtful look on my face and huffs a withering sigh. "Contrary to what fantasy universe you grew up in, Holly, nobody does good deeds just because they feel like it. Not unless there's something in it for them," Ray mentions as if he believes it's too good to be true. "This could be your big break, Holly," he says the words to entice me, and it works.

I let that settle in the air between us. My big break. It's what I've always dreamed about. If The Workshop was using dirty money, and I rumble them, this could skyrocket my career.

"So, you want me to dig up the dirt on this guy and expose him to the world?" I ask, and Ray nods in affirmation.

"There's a press conference on Saturday, down at the Grande Pavilion." The Grande Pavilion is a theatre set by the waterside and plays host to huge corporate events. "That's when he'll reveal his identity. I bet he's a mobster," Ray scrunches his face as he says it. "I'm letting you go to the conference instead of Sasha. You'll get to ask the first question. As I said, it's your big break. I don't offer chances like this to just anyone. Only the ones who have bright futures in this industry. So, what do you say?"

I feel like I'm making a deal with the Devil. But I have a kid to feed. I'll do anything to provide for my son. Even if it means selling out Santa, or whoever this guy is. "Yes," I reply. "Oh my God, Mr. Frost. Thank you for this opportunity."
Ray gathers his files from that table, then he glances up at me through the tendrils of hair that fall in front of his eyes. Against my better judgment, my heart does a girly flip, and I mentally curse myself for being an office sheep. I don't want to follow the flock into Ray's slaughterhouse, I mean bed. I have a job to do. I'm here to work, and that's it.

Chapter 6

Holly

Ray stops me before I punch out for the evening and introduces me to a cameraman named Jason. I recognize him from when I first started working here, and vaguely remember he used to be Sasha's cameraman before she refused to work with him again.
Jason flashes an easy smile and reaches out to shake my hand. "It's a pleasure to be working with you, Holly," he says, flashing a dazzling set of white teeth. My pale hand contrasts against his dark skin, soft and warm. Not a nervous handshake like mine. His handshake oozes confidence. He smells good too. I

notice he's wearing sneakers with a suit, and I like his casual sense of style. It suits him. He seems like a down-to-earth guy. "Your face is so familiar." Jason's brown eyes twitch as he remembers me. I'm always running errands, and he's usually out somewhere filming, doing a job he loves. "We were both hired on the same day, am I right?" He checks to see if his facts are straight before assuming.

"Yeah, that's right," I reply, smiling back at him. "How come it didn't work out with Sasha?" I find myself asking. He seems like such a sweetheart. If he was terrible at his job, Ray would have fired him on the spot. Jason flashes Ray a knowing look, one that makes me think I have gotten my wires crossed. It's just as I thought, Jason isn't the problem. Sasha is.

"She's a nightmare," Jason tells me, to which Ray chortles.

"I'll leave you guys to it," Ray says, jingling his car keys as he leaves.

Jason glances around to check no one is within earshot. "Honestly, Sasha drives me crazy. You're not friends with her, are you?" He double-checks.

I chuckle at that. "God, no. She hates me."

"Sasha hates everybody," Jason firmly states. "Except for Ray. She thinks he's gonna catapult her into stardom." He makes an amused snort as if he knows differently.

We reach the elevators and Jason presses the button. People pile into the first one, so we hold back and wait for the second one to arrive.

"They've slept together then," I ask, to which Jason vigorously nods his head.

"Yeah, Ray and the rest of the guys in the building," he mentions, his voice tinged with regret.

"Oh, not you too," I say, just as the elevator doors open.

Jason winces sheepishly. "It was one time, and —" he scrubs his hand over his face, his blush staining his dark cheeks with embarrassment. "It's something I'd like to forget. How about you? Have you got any office tales to share?"

The elevator doors close as Jason presses the button for the ground floor and the confined box descends, leaving my empty stomach behind.

"Nope, not me," I reply. "My conscience is clear."

Jason chuckles. "Well, I'm taking a shot at redemption. I prefer to be on the nice list as opposed to the naughty one." He winks. "I'm hoping we'll make a great team, and that I'll still have a job in the New Year." His tone grows serious, and I can relate to that. I'm scared of losing this job. I can't afford to get fired.

"Me too," I agree, meeting his smile. "It's good to have at least one friend in this place. I feel like a small fish swimming in a shark tank."

"Girl, me too," he replies, exhaling a sigh.

The doors open and we walk out into the wide-open space of the entrance hall, then through the revolving glass door into the bitter cold. Jason stops as I get to my car, thrusting his hands inside his trouser pockets to keep them warm. A dusting of snow whirls past my face in a tiny flurry, then seconds later, more appears, fluttering from the sky like sugar dust.

"Snow, in Port Sunshine?" Jason glances heavenward and huffs a disbelieving smile. "No way." He chuckles. I get a rush of excitement from somewhere deep inside me like my inner child wants to burst free and squeal jubilantly, hoping it will gather mass and stick so I can build a snowman with Nicky.

"Oh, wow, this is a first," I gush. "My son will love this. He was too young to appreciate it when we lived in New York. He's four, and he's obsessed with

Christmas. But I guess all kids are."

"My niece is the same age," Jason tells me. "She's written a list to Santa, and it's as long as my arm. My sister is taking her to the grotto tomorrow. Maybe we can meet up with them afterward and go for some hot chocolate." He blanches as soon as he says it like he doesn't want it to sound like he's asking me out on a date. "I mean, it would be nice for the kids. I'm not trying to make it weird or anything. It'll be you, Mr. Harper, your son, my sis, my niece, and me. Work doesn't always have to be boring."

"Nice save," I joke with him. "But there is no Mr. Harper," I say with a melancholy tone. "I'm a single mom. Nicky has never met his father. Not through my doing. It was a one-night thing."

Jason flashes a sympathetic smile that reassures me. "Well, it sounds to me that Nicky is doing just fine with having a supermom like you. We're gonna smash this story up," Jason says with confidence. "I'll admit, I'm a little skeptical that our guy is a gangster, but either way, we're gonna give the world an awesome story. What do you say, partner? Are you ready to step up and take the world by storm?"

I'm still on the fence about the whole wreck Christmas vendetta that Ray has going on, and it seems to me that Jason is on the same wavelength as I am. If we don't find any dirt on the mystery man at The Workshop, then we can still gain ratings by putting on a show. A spectacular show. News channels do it all the time. They find some other gimmick to entice viewers to watch. This is as much my big break as it is Jason's, and I'm glad that we're in this together.

I grinned, slapping my palm against Jason's to seal the deal. "We gotta talk to Ray and persuade him to give us some decent airtime. If we're going to do this, we gotta gain the public's interest."

"Yeah, it'll be such a shame to put all this effort into something if nothing becomes of it," Jason agrees. "Ray will ditch the story if we don't find any incriminating evidence against The Workshop, which I doubt we'll find. As much as it'll pain him, he'll need to agree to let us run a story from now until Christmas Eve. Everybody loves Christmas; they'll love tuning in to watch your daily report."

I roll my eyes dramatically. "I wouldn't go as far to say everybody Loves Christmas, Jason. I'm interested in reporting about the real struggles of Christmas. There are a lot of lonely people out there. People who are trying to make ends meet. There's a darker side to the holidays that gets swept to one side. Let's use this opportunity to do something good. Remind people that sharing really is about caring, and it's not about personal gain, selfishness, or greed. If The CEO does turn out to be a crook, at least the citizens of Port Sunshine will know they can trust us to let the truth shine through."

"What are you thinking?" Jason asks curiously.

It's freezing now. I'm losing the sensation in the tips of my toes. My teeth are chattering, and I stomp my feet on the parking lot to keep my blood flowing.

"I'm thinking, we report about the grotto, the store, and their charity agenda, but we also report on the food bank, the homeless shelter, and all the local charities who support vulnerable people within the community. That way, we still have something good to overshadow the bad. Breaking people's spirits doesn't sit right with me, Jason. But reporting the truth does."

Jason and I part ways before we turn into human popsicles. It takes me a while to scrape the ice from my windshield and defrost the car. The drive home is hindered by the rush-hour traffic, and I'm forced to endure back-to-back Christmas songs on the radio. My wiper blades clear the snow from my windshield making the dazzling brake lights from the car in front light up my dash bright red. The repetition of stop, start, stop, start, is using way too much gas, and by the time I arrive home, I just want to crawl to my bed and sleep. But I can't. I haven't seen Nicky since I took him to school this morning. He greets me in the hall with his arms open wide.

"Mommy!" he exclaims, rushing to hug me. "Grandma made cookies."

I lift Nicky and hoist him onto my hip. This enables me to multitask. I dump my purse, kick off my shoes, and toss my coat onto the hook like a game of hoopla as I carry him around with me.

"Guess what happened at school today, Mommy?" Nicky says, excited to tell me.

"Did you cut snowflake decorations out of paper? Or did you make a Christmas card?" I ask, guessing.

Nicky shakes his head. "Nope, we still have to do all that, Mommy. But Miss Littlemore picked me to play Santa in the Nativity."

I give an exaggerated gasp of surprise. "Wow, that's awesome. But did she say you could be Santa, just so you'd stop trying to make changes to the play?"

Nicky grins, and I know I'm right. I carry him into the living room and through to the kitchenette. Our studio apartment flows into one big living space, and I find my mom rolling out some cookie dough on the countertop. She sees me and smiles.

"Hey, I saved you some dinner. It just needs reheating," she says.

"Thanks, Mom, I'm starving," I reply gratefully.

She casts me a disapproving frown. "You shouldn't skip meals, Holly. Your body can't run on empty."
"Mom, I didn't have time to grab a sandwich on the way to work," I tell her. "I was running late this morning."

Mom washes the dough from her fingers and dries her hands on a dishtowel. Nicky wriggles in my arms, wanting to get down, so I put him down and he climbs on the stool at the breakfast bar, rolls up his sleeves, and begins cutting out shapes in the dough with cookie cutters.
"Have you seen the snow?" I ask him, pointing to the window.
Nicky nods. "Uh-huh," he replies, busy making cookies.
"It's beginning to feel a lot like Christmas," Mom says, quoting the Bing Crosby lyric.
Nicky glances up at her and smiles, whereas I internally groan.
"It'll feel more like Christmas when you see Santa tomorrow," I tell Nicky, seeing his face light up like a Christmas tree.
"Really? We're going to see Santa. The real Santa!" he asks, awed by the idea of that.
I cringe a little, hating the fact that I'm lying to my son. There is no Santa. The guy he's going to see is just a store employee who gets to dress up in a costume. So, I do what my mom did for me when I was his age, I smile brightly and lie through my teeth.
"You bet, he's the real Santa," I tell him, holding the heavy smile upon my face. "He has real elves too."

Nicky beams, and I see the sparkle in his eyes that reminds me of Nick.

Chapter 7

44

Nick

Bernard bursts through the door and drops a newspaper on my desk. "Look at what they're saying, Santa has arrived early this year," he announces proudly.
I click off the page I'm looking at, then turn my computer screen away from Bernard's line of sight. He doesn't need to know what I'm looking at. He'll lecture me about losing focus, and how everything is riding on our stores being successful – blah, blah, blah. I know how important this year is. I don't need people ramming it down my throat.
"I'm not Santa yet. That's still my grandfather's job," I point out, lounging back in my chair.
Bernard swats his hand in dismissal. "Oh, mistletoe. You're as good as Santa already. This will be is his last year flying the sleigh."

It was true. My grandpa announced to everyone that he was stepping down after Christmas, and I would be stepping into his big black boots. We have so much to do in the run-up to the big day. My schedule is packed full of meetings, charity events, television, and press interviews. I've barely had the time to rest. But when I'm not working, I spend all my time trying to find Holly. Well, that's what I was doing right before Bernard barged in here and startled me.
"You know —" Bernard eyes me with scrutiny, "you could try to look more enthusiastic."
He tries to peek at my computer screen, but all he sees is a reindeer screensaver.
"I'm delighted," I reply, coming off as sarcastic, but that isn't my intention. Bernard is not an idiot. He sees right through my façade. The guilt crashes over me

and millions of vulnerable children flash through my mind's eye, churning my stomach with remorse. Their needs take priority over mine. How dare I wallow in self-pity when children are starving, people have lost their homes, their jobs, and some are left with nothing. I shake away the notion and rethink my response. "Honestly, I am. I'm so completely dedicated to this job. I can't wait to make things better. It's just –" my voice trails off, betraying the way I feel, and Bernard can tell something is eating at me, and it's not acid reflux from eating too many mince pies.

"Holly," he says, finishing my sentence.
Her name hangs there like an invisible weight around my heart.
I swallow hard and nod. "Yeah . . . I tried calling her, but her phone number is no longer in service. So, I did the next best thing and reached out to her mom, but no answer. I even called the garage, hoping to talk to Hazel, but all I got was a cold reply from some girl named Meredith, telling me that Holly doesn't live with them anymore, and never to call back."
Bernard frowns, then taps his chin as he thinks. "Hm, that's strange. If Holly moved, Santa would know about it. He knows where everyone lives."
My eyes twitch questioningly. "So, you think they're lying to me about Holly's whereabouts? Why would they do that?"
Bernard shoots me a critical look as if to say, "do you really need to ask?" And I sigh exhaustedly, knowing he's right. I don't deserve their help. Why would they want me anywhere near Holly after I abandoned her?
"Things have a strange way of working themselves out," Bernard tells me, always the voice of optimism. "If you want my advice, focus on the press conference

tomorrow. If Holly watches the news, she's bound to see you on TV. Maybe you won't have to go to her; she'll come to you."

I huff a pessimistic sigh. "I hope so." Maybe it's the only way I will know for sure if she's still interested in me. It doesn't mean I'll stop looking for her. Nothing will stop me from trying to make amends with her. But I need to change the subject because I'm choking up. "How's the grotto coming along?" I ask, hoping that everything is running smoothly. "Have the Norwegian spruces arrived that I ordered? I hope Gramps knows not to eat the props. You did tell him the gingerbread houses are just for show, right?"

Bernard slumps all his weight onto one foot, placing his hand on his hip. "Stop fussing. Of course, he knows. He's not an idiot, Nick."

I get up and drag my suit jacket from the back of my swivel chair. "Good. I want everything to be perfect for the opening night. For once, the kids who come to see Santa will get to meet the real Santa, and not just some dude in a fake beard who passed the mandatory police check."

Bernard grabs my notes from the desk and thrusts them under my nose. "Don't forget your speech for tomorrow," he reminds me. "You ought to memorize it exactly how we wrote it, do you hear me?"

I take the papers, roll them up, then shove them inside my jacket pocket. "Don't worry. I won't blow the family secret," I promise.

Bernard makes a doubtful snort as I turn around to leave. My office is on the top floor of the toy store, and I'm proud to say, it's the biggest and most extraordinary toy store I've ever seen – almost as wonderful as the real Santa's workshop. I want people to walk through the doors tomorrow and feel the magic inside these walls. It's got to be perfect. Everything's got to be just right. There's a world of wonders to explore on each of the seven floors. The shelves have been crammed full of all the latest toys, down to the most traditional classics. I can't wait to cut the red tape and give people a taste of my homeland without revealing too much of it, just enough to leave them wondering. It's what will keep the magic alive. The human workers are busy putting the finishing touches to the décor, making sure every bulb lights up, and every bauble is positioned perfectly so. I feel a proud sense of achievement for accomplishing this. We're going to do so much good giving back to worthy causes. Not just in this community, but everywhere, all over the world.

"Goodnight, Mr. Christmas," a male member of staff says as he holds the door for me to leave.

"Good night, Rory," I reply, without even glancing at his nametag.

I pause, my eyes bulging wide with surprise. This has never happened to me before. My eyes glance down at the rectangular golden nametag pinned to his uniform and notice his name is Rory – and I don't know how I knew that . . . I just did. I look around the store, confident that I know everybody's name. The feeling is overwhelming, and I huff a stunned smile. It's already happening. My grandfather's magic is transferring over to me. I'm becoming Santa.

Rory flashes a toothy smile as he locks the door behind me. It's late. All the stores are closed, but the Christmas lights are left on to illuminate the empty streets. Snow flutters from the sky in coin-size clumps, covering everything in a blanket of white. It's like being stuck inside a giant snow globe.

The snow globe.

If I had access to it, I could pinpoint Holly's whereabouts. But then I remember Bernard's words, knowing only too well that magic will not solve all my problems. If I risk going back to the North Pole, I may have to wait another year until I can return, and I don't want that. This is my chance to set things right and be the man I was born to be. I just hope I get my Christmas wish this year – that I've been good enough to deserve it. Something shuffles in a store doorway, and I glance down to see a cardboard sheet move. It's covered in snow, and that's not all . . . I think there's someone underneath it.

"Excuse me?" I say, not wanting to startle whoever it was by pulling away their shelter.
The cardboard lifts at one corner, and I see a middle-aged African American man cocooned in a sleeping bag. He's wearing layers of dirty clothing, and an old beanie hat and gloves. He cracks one eye open, his haggard face scrunched with fatigue.
"I'm not botherin' anyone," he gruffs. "I'll move first thing tomorrow."
"That's not what I was going to ask, Eddie," I say, baffling him as to how I know his name.
This makes him sit up and take notice. I see the panic in his eyes, not wanting any trouble.

"Are you a cop?" he asks with an air of distrust. "I didn't steal anything. The restaurant was throwing food in the trash. Better in my belly, than to leave it for the rats."

His words make me wince. "No, Eddie, I'm not a cop." He scoots away from me as I crouch down to talk to him. "Well, who in the hell are you then, and how do you know my name?"

"I'm a friend," I tell him, willing him to trust me.

He eyes me warily, and I can tell I'm making him feel threatened, which isn't my intention. So, I stand up and take a step back to give him some space. This seems to work because his posture relaxes.

"You're not from around here, are you?" Eddie asks, his questioning squint telling me he knows there's something amiss. "You're different. Are you sure you're a friend? I don't owe you money, do I?"

I chuckle at that. "You don't owe me anything, but maybe we could help each other out." I offer him my hand to help him to his feet, and Eddie takes it, finding it difficult to stand. He clutches his back with a grimace on his face, his joints seizing up from the cold.

"I'm not doing anything illegal," he tells me.

I blanch at that. "I know. I'm not saying you are, but I am offering you an honest job and a warm place to stay," I'm quick to clarify. "You'll freeze to death if you stay out here tonight. You look like you could use a decent meal and some clean clothes."

Eddie nods soberly. "That's kind of you. I appreciate it. The shelter was full tonight. I was late getting there, but at least some other guy will get a comfortable bed for the night." He tries to sound upbeat. "How do you know my name?" he asks again cautiously.

"I know everybody's name," I reply, helping him gather his belongings from inside the store doorway. I could tell it didn't sit right with him, and I owed him a reasonable explanation. "I donate to the shelter and I saw you there the other night and overheard you giving your name to the guy on the door. I'm Nick by the way. The CEO of the Workshop." I gesture at the store behind us.

Eddie nods with acceptance. "Ah, that explains it then. For a second there, I thought you were from the IRS." He laughs, then splutters into a coughing fit.

I help carry his belonging to the undercover parking lot where I parked my car, then shove everything into the trunk. Eddie climbs into the passenger seat and blows into his gloved hands. It's freezing. I fire the engine and wait for the blowers to heat up. Then I turn on the heated seats.

"Do you have family in Port Sunshine?" I ask curiously.

Eddie lets out a long sigh. "Yeah, but I can't face them. I let them both down so badly when their mom died. I didn't handle things as well as I should have."

"You got kids?" I reply, interested to learn more.

"Grown-up kids," Eddie corrects me. "One has a kid of her own to worry about. I don't even know if she had a boy or a girl. How bad is that? And my son went to media school — he was always making home videos — Jason is a talented man, and I'm proud of him," he tells me, gushing with pride. Then his expression darkens, drawing his brows together in a sorrowful frown. "He doesn't need an old bum like me showing up on his doorstep, dragging him down." He looks at his hands and I hear the shame in his voice as he mutters, "It's better that I stay away. Everything I touch turns to crap."

I drive out of the parking lot and steer us through the glittering streets. "Christmas is a time for miracles," I tell him, quoting Bernard's words. "Maybe we can both figure out a way to make amends with the people we love."

Eddie doesn't argue with that, which tells me he's all for grasping a second chance at life. You've just got to want it badly enough — because what if you regret not trying?

"What did you do for work before?" I ask, cutting my sentence short. I was about to add, "*before you ended up on the streets*", but I could tell his past was a sore subject. It was easier to bring up something other than his family.

"I was a manager of a hardware store. Why? What sort of job do you have in mind for me?" he asks, side-eyeing me.
I didn't want this to sound like a prank, so I chose my next words wisely. "I need someone to run the toy store while I'm away on business excursions. I'll be gone for several months of the year, so I need someone who knows how to manage a workforce. And as you have managerial experience, you're the ideal guy for the job."

"Are you shitting me?" Eddie stammers. "You want me to run the store?" He laughs with disbelief. "If I'm hallucinating, this is one heck of a blackout."

I chuckle. "It's not. It's real. The job is yours if you want it."

"Hell yeah, I want it," Eddie rushes to accept my offer.

As of next year, I'll be far too busy at the North Pole. I won't have time to manage the flagship store. Not if I'm Santa. But for some reason, I know Eddie was in the wrong place at the right time. He and I were supposed to meet. His Christmas wish was as strong as mine.

Chapter 8

The previous evening I had the most peculiar dream. It was so abnormal. Scratch was in it, and we were clasping hands, strolling through the snow. He went to me, his eyes sparkling underneath the variety of multi-shaded pixie lights. He inclined down to kiss me . . . also I rose on my toes to kiss him back, all my displeasure neglected, covered underneath the energy that he was here with me, he'd return for me. Also a hot wet sensation lapped at my face, the tyrannical smell of canine bread rolls overwhelmed the memory of his cinnamon zest cologne. As my eyelids shudder, the picture blurs, alongside the memory of what he looked like, how great he smelled, how I used to feel – still feel. Presently all I'm left with is a feeling of misfortune, an immense void, not an incredible method for beginning my day.

"Greg," I protest, stroking my unwavering Dachshund. He barks, then, at that point, does a lap of honor around my head. "Fine, I'm getting up." Because assuming that I don't, he'll pee by the entryway.

"Mama!" Nicky shouts to me as he comes jumping into my room, skips on the bed, and plunges underneath the blanket.

"You're feeling lively," I say, snuggling him.

"The present the day we meet Santa!" he answers energetically.

I laugh. "It's not until this evening, Munchkin."

Nicky indulgences back the blanket, letting out all the glow. "We should eat, then, at that point, watch a Christmas film," he recommends.

I moan, then, at that point, hesitantly get up and scour the rest from my eyes. "Fine . . . however, you're not having treats for breakfast."

"I'll have Elf grain then, at that point," Nicky responses rapidly.

Not that I need to get up at the butt break of day, yet I don't have a lot of decision with an over-invigorated youngster, and a canine with a full bladder in the house. I let Greg out to pee, then, at that point, fix Nicky some grain as my espresso brews. Since the canine is settled, moving around underneath the Christmas tree, we're ready to shower, clean our teeth, and style our hair. Nicky's hair won't tame however much I brush it down. He's so similar to Nick, it alarms me. He puts on his Christmas jumper, and I put on a sewed cream dress I purchased in the deals. It has an elasticated belt with a gold catch at the front. I group it with my beloved dark slouch boots and a couple of transparent leggings. It isn't happy, however essentially it will keep me warm.

"We have ages to pause," I remind Nicky. "How would it be advisable for us we deal with kill some time."

I lament posing the inquiry as Nicky jumps for the TV remote. "We should watch a Christmas film," he answers with an excessive lot of energy during the current hour of the morning. I really want essentially one more three espressos fuel me for the remainder of the day.

Nicky picks an endearing film about a young lady who doesn't have a mother. Her Christmas wish is for her dad to find love once more, and the storyline hits excessively near and dear. I can't watch it through the tears in my eyes. The apparition of scratch actually gauges weighty at the forefront of my thoughts later that lovely dream. Damn him. Indeed, even Greg can detect the change in my mind-set and cuddles next to me. I really want some enjoyable to take my brain off things. Perhaps I'll luck out at the workplace Christmas celebration and have a merry hurl with the task fellow, or possibly I'll discard my ethical compass and offer an evening of sizzling enthusiasm with Ray. Or on the other hand not. All I know is . . . I really want to get laid. This can't be my life, watching messy low-financial plan Christmas films and wishing they'd work out as expected."Mother," Nicky says, shaking me. "The film finished. Are you OK?" he asks, his foreheads dimpling with concern.

My eyelids shudder as I think about a reason. He found me sulking once more. It generally occurs around this season. I can't resist. There's no getting away from the recollections that return flooding, all due to the name Christmas.

"No doubt, I recently recalled that, I didn't compose my shopping list," I say, tapping my head as though the suspected abruptly happens to me.

Nicky's eyes broaden and he sucks in a pant of acknowledgment. "Oh goodness, I didn't compose my letter for Santa," he specifies, running off to get his scratch pad and pen.

I roll off the sofa and stretch my arms with a yawn. The canine leaps onto the carpet and flounders somewhere around the window divider to gaze outside. Our road is unrecognizable; snow takes care of everything, helping me to remember a scene from a Christmas card.

"Momma needs more espresso," I murmur, then, at that point, add, "and potentially something more grounded the subsequent it goes dim this evening."

Jason and I have such a huge amount to do, and the strain is on us to convey a considerable story on Christmas Eve. The poop is getting genuine – similarly as genuine as the lease that is expected, and every one of the bills I must compensation. I just had a few things left to purchase on Nicky's current rundown. He never requests a lot, yet I generally search around to top it up. He's thankful for whatever he gets.

Nicky sits at the morning meal bar as he composes the letter, then, at that point, seals it in a red envelope that has the Workshop stamp imprinted onto it. The store sent them out to every one of the schools in the space so the children could compose a letter to Santa and get an answer by Christmas Eve. It's a business contrivance, yet a thoroughly examined one no different either way. Their advertising group merits a gesture of congratulations for concocting one more method for tricking individuals into their store. As though the announcements and TV plugs aren't sufficient.

"I'm done," Nicky declares, having fixed the envelope with a gingerbread man sticker. "You ought to do yours, Mom."

I feign exacerbation with entertainment. "Honey, Santa knows there's nothing I need in excess of a serene Christmas. However, to send me a culinary specialist to prepare me supper, then, at that point, I won't deny that."

Nicky breathes out a mournful moan. "For what reason would you confirm or deny that you are amped up for Christmas, Mom? You generally need it to be over before it's started? You never chime in to the Christmas songs at the faith gathering," he says critically, making me recoil since it's valid. I just ever lip-synchronize. "You gripe the embellishments mess the condo," he added, and I was unable to contend with him since that was likewise evident. "You never chuckle at the jokes in the Christmas saltines," he denounces.

I raise my finger in the air. "Hello – for all intents and purposes, nobody at any point chuckles at the jokes, their weak," I say protectively.

Nicky glowers, folding his arms. "You're a Christmas Grinch, simply let it be known," he affronts me, and it hits me like a sock in the stomach since I object to that comment. I'm not a Grinch. I simply don't want to bounce into Christmas as energetically as certain individuals. I like to stall.

"I've met the Grinch," I tell Nicky. "Truly, I work for him. He's my chief – and he and I are not all that much. He despises Christmas," I notice, hearing Nicky heave with shock. "He doesn't have a tree like this one," I say, signaling at the fake tree toward the side of our room that we've enriched with red and gold doodads and gleaming lights. Nicky's custom made holy messenger is roosted on the highest point of it with a smiley face, considering she has a tree tip slammed up her butt.Nicky scrunches his lips as he might suspect. "This is a direct result of my father, isn't it?" he mutters, picking at the sleeve of his sweater. "You generally try to avoid Christmas since it helps you to remember him."

Culpability shoots through my heart and annihilates all the other things. "Where did you hear that?"

Nicky meets my look and I see the misery and disarray behind his eyes. I've just at any point spoken momentarily about Nick each time he asked, yet I generally discover some method of changing the subject. It's just normal for him to be curious with regards to his father. He realizes Nick's last name is Christmas, and that is the reason he cherishes special times of year to such an extent. Possibly I should continue the quest for the wellbeing of him for Nicky. He doesn't need me, however he should know Nicky. I'm simply frightened he may dismiss him. I would rather do nothing that will hurt my child. Knowing his dad – not knowing his dad – what the heck do I do? How might I make this right? I want a Christmas marvel like the one from the film, where I award a wish and everything we could ever hope for work out as expected.

"Grandmother told me. She said at whatever point you think about my father you get pitiful," Nicky murmurs a delicate answer.

I squat to Nicky's level and take his hands in mine, asking him to check out me. "Please accept my apologies. I vow not to be a Christmas Grinch. For what reason don't we do some great stuff together?"

"Like go to the skating park?" Nicky wheezes joyfully. "Also have a snowball battle?"

Falling on my butt exposed and being pelted with ice isn't actually a good time for me, yet in the event that it satisfies Nicky then, at that point, I'm holding nothing back.

"Indeed, why not?" I laugh. "I'm on a Christmas mission this year, however I could utilize a little assistance to view as the wizardry

.

Nicky grins. "To observe the wizardry, you should converse with Santa. He knows where it is. He knows it all."

I look at my watch and notice the time. "Indeed, talking about time – it's an ideal opportunity to take off. Go get your jacket, and remember your cap and gloves. It's virus out."

Nicky runs around to prepare, and I really take a look at my tote to ensure I have the tickets. I send a message to Jason, telling him that we're leaving, letting him know where to meet. He answers with a thumb's up emoticon and a smiley face.

"Remember your letter to Santa," I remind Nicky.

He taps his jacket pocket. "Got it."

"On the off chance that you really want to pee, go now," I say, realizing he'll report he wants to go two minutes into the excursion. He generally does.

Nicky ponders this, then, at that point, shakes his head. "I'm completely fine."

I put on my cap and coat, and toss a cashmere scarf around my neck, and I'm all set. Greg stretches and yawns then he takes a gander at me with dismal eyes for leaving him home.

"We'll be back soon, Greg," I say warmly. "They don't permit canines at the toy store."

I lock the entryway behind us. Nicky follows me down to the vehicle and moves onto the secondary lounge as I clear the snow from the windshield and thump what I can from the rooftop. I affix his tackle and check it's protected. He's shaking with fervor, and I can't move past how cheerful it causes me to feel just to see him like this. As far as I might be concerned, this is what's really going on with it. It merits all the promotion, all the quarrel, and all the disarray just to see him grin. Assuming I could bottle Nicky's Christmas soul, it would sell for millions.

The street into town is rushed and it's all gratitude to the launch of the new toy store, The Workshop. Individuals are out in huge numbers Christmas shopping, kids are queueing with their folks to see Santa, and couples are strolling affectionately intertwined around the merry market slows down, purchasing tailor made presents and treats. In the wake of circumnavigating the stuffed parking area, somebody moves and empowers me to hop into the empty space. We're here, and I'm becoming energized for Nicky. He holds my hand as I lead him through the clamoring roads. The smell of simmered pork and fruit purée floats over from the hoard cook cabin, and my mouth salivates lavishly. I'm as of now contemplating lunch, however assuming we don't join the line currently, we're probably going to miss our timeslot.

"Holly!" I hear my name being called from across the road and go to see Jason jarring through the group with a young lady sticking to his hand. I can see the family likeness in the lady remaining close to them and I figure she's Jason's sister. They delay until it's protected to cross, then, at that point, hustle over to welcome us.

"Thea, this is Holly," Jason presents us, and we shake hands, "and this is my sister, Nakeisha, however we call her Keisha for short. Furthermore this is my niece, Natalia. Natalia is a Christmas child. She'll praise her fifth birthday celebration this year."

Nicky looks around at them and waves modestly. "Hey, Nata," he says. "I like your Christmas dress," he praises her red plaid dress and matching coat. Her dark braids stick out from underneath her red beret and are tied off at the finishes with gold wafer bows. She rearranges her gleaming dark boots through the snow, her timid grin twisting her lips as she answers, "Much appreciated, my father got it for me."

"All things considered, it's exquisite," I tell her. "He has an extraordinary eye for design. I wish my father did." Natalia is such the best young lady, the picture of her mother. I recall Nicky letting me know he made a companion at preschool, and presently I on second thought, her name rings a bell.

"Marcus wants to be here," Keisha says affectionately. "Yet, he needs to work. He runs a youngsters' design store across town called Bows and Belles."

"Really?" My temples hit my hairline since I love that store. "I purchase all Nicky's garments from that point. I never go elsewhere."

"I perceive the coat," Kiesha remarks.

Jason inclines nearer to his sister. "Does this mean my companion can get a rebate?" he murmurs from the edge of his mouth.

Kiesha smiles. "Obviously. In any case, in the event that you need a few gifts, possibly Nicky could demonstrate some garments close by Natalia for the spring assortment?"

I hold my hands at my sides. "You had me at gifts. I could utilize all the assist I with canning get. Kids aren't modest."

"I'm trusting Ray sees our latent capacity and gives us more broadcast appointment later this," Jason says, acquiring a gesture from me.

"Assuming we come up bests with this story, possibly there'll be a huge Christmas reward in our next check?" I say ideally, however I question we'll have the option to press one more dime from Ebenezer Scrooge. Beam possibly pays additional when he's receiving sexual blessings in return.

The snow crunches underneath our feet as we stand by in line. I fish the tickets from my tote, and Keisha does likewise. Jason tells me he reserved a bodycam and a mouthpiece inside the buttonholes of his jacket. He's completely wired up and all set. This leaves me allowed to pose some pivotal inquiries. There's a lot of staff here on the first day of the season. Someone will undoubtedly know some things about the proprietor. We as a whole are astonished he isn't here to cut the administrative noise, an old woman named Mary does it. She's dressed like Mother Christmas and looks genuine as well. I ascend on my pussyfoots and friend over the group. I can't see a lot, simply tufts of buildup from breathed out breath. It's freezing outside. The line moves gradually, then, at that point, following twenty minutes of holding up vulnerable, we venture inside the store, and it knocks my socks off. I feel the invigoration hurrying through me like we've recently ventured through a gateway into Lapland. My eyes extend as I drink in the view, and it resembles I'm five years of age once more.

"Goodness," I mumble, awed by the remarkable toy store.

    The End..

9 7 9 8 7 8 7 8 7 0 9 6 1